WRITTEN BY **Robert Quackenbush** • ILLUSTRATED BY **Yan Nascimbene**

# First Grade Jitters

**HARPER**
*An Imprint of HarperCollinsPublishers*

First for Piet, and now for Aidan
—R.Q.

To Little Aldo
—Y.N.

First Grade Jitters
Text copyright © 1982, 2010 by Robert Quackenbush
Illustrations copyright © 2010 by Yan Nascimbene

Library of Congress Cataloging-in-Publication Data
Quackenbush, Robert M.
     First grade jitters / written by Robert Quackenbush ; illustrated by Yan Nascimbene. — 1st ed.
         p.       cm.
     Summary: A small boy wonders what first grade will be like but is not sure that he wants to find out.
     ISBN 978-0-06-077632-9
     [1. Schools—Fiction.]   I. Nascimbene, Yan, ill.   II. Title.
PZ7.Q16Fi   2010                                          2009007290
[E]—dc22                                                  CIP
                                                         AC

Typography by Jeanne L. Hogle
15  16   LEO   10  9  8  7  6
❖
Newly illustrated edition

Mom says I have first grade jitters.
Dad says I am cranky and not myself.

It's not true.

I am the same as always.

I still watch TV.
I still draw pictures.
I still play with my soldiers.
So what if I don't feel like eating?

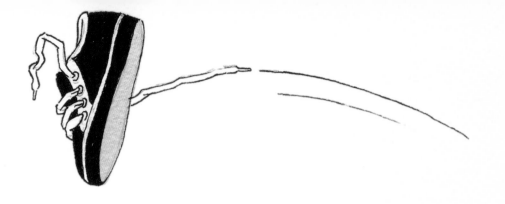

So what if I hollered and kicked when Mom took me to the store to buy new shoes for school?

School doesn't worry me.
Last year I had a lot of fun there,
playing blocks with Tammy, Kevin,
and Jason.
I was in Kindergarten then.

Well, maybe I do think a little about first grade
and wonder what it will be like.

just a little.

Things like will Tammy and
Kevin and Jason be there?
They've been away all
summer.

And I wonder what the
teacher will be like.
    I might have to read or spell.
    Or maybe do some arithmetic.
    I don't know how to do any of
those things.

What then?

And what if I can't
understand anything the
teacher says?
She might say, "Oogly, boogly."
When I ask her what that
means, she might answer,
"Muncha, chumba, zeglipo."

Now I'm scared.
I think I'll go to bed.
And stay there.

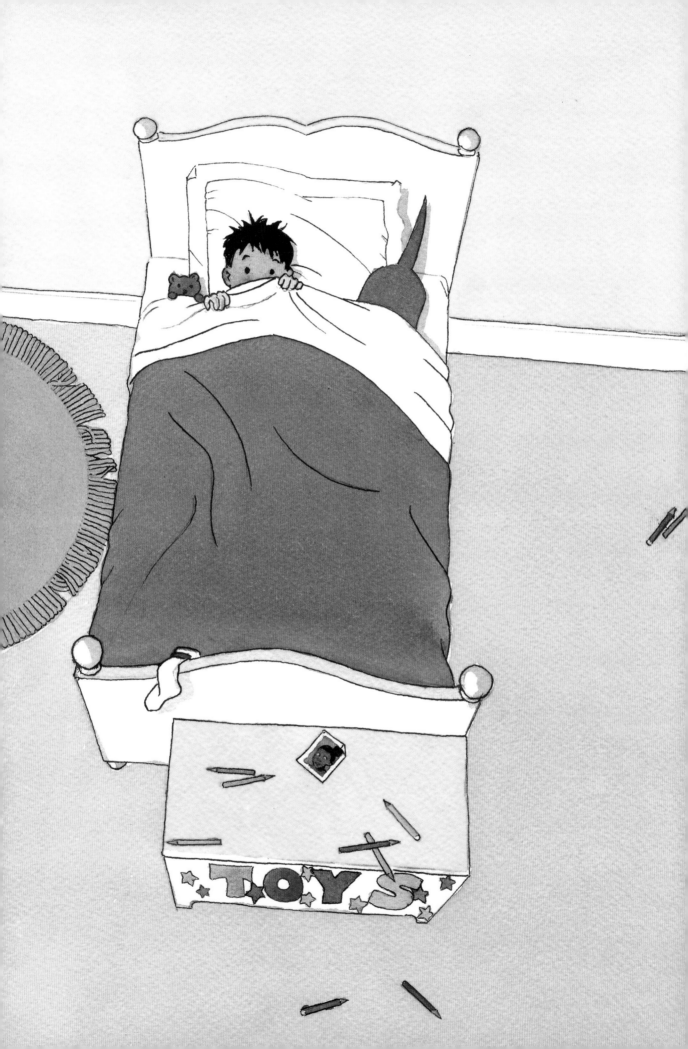

"What's the matter, Aidan?" Mom asks. "Don't you feel well?"

"It's my leg," I tell her. "I can't walk."

"That's too bad," Mom says. "I hope it will be better before school starts."

"I don't think so," I say.

Just then, the phone rings.
Mom answers it.
"It's for you," she says.
I take the phone.

It's Tammy calling!
"Where have you been all summer?" I ask.
"At my grandpa and grandma's,"
answers Tammy. "Can I come over and play?"
Tammy comes over and we play with my blocks.

Later, Jason calls.

Then Kevin.

They come over, too.

Tammy tells us that she met our teacher
today when she was with her mom at the
supermarket. "Her name is Miss Welsh,"
says Tammy. "And she's nice!"

I ask Tammy, "Did Miss Welsh want to know if you could read and write and do math?"

"Of course not, silly," answers Tammy. "She knows I can't do those things. That's what she's going to be teaching us."

I'm feeling better inside.

I ask Tammy, "And did Miss Welsh talk in a way you couldn't understand? Did she say *muncha, chumba,* or *zeglipo?*"

"No!" Tammy shouts, laughing. "She talks like we do."

My jitters are gone!

I say, "Let's play big yellow school bus, and I'll be the driver."

And we did.